To:

WITHDRAWN

From:

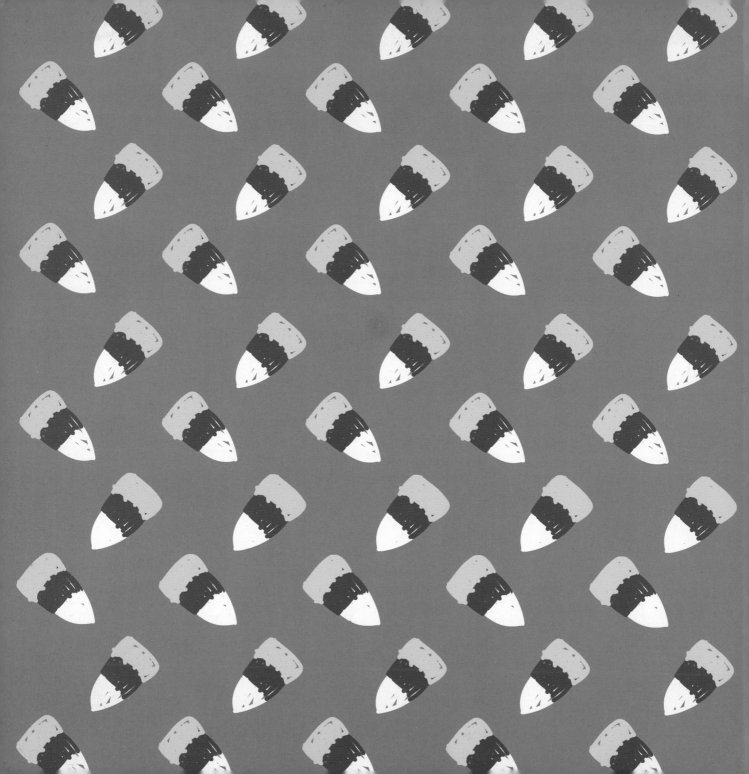

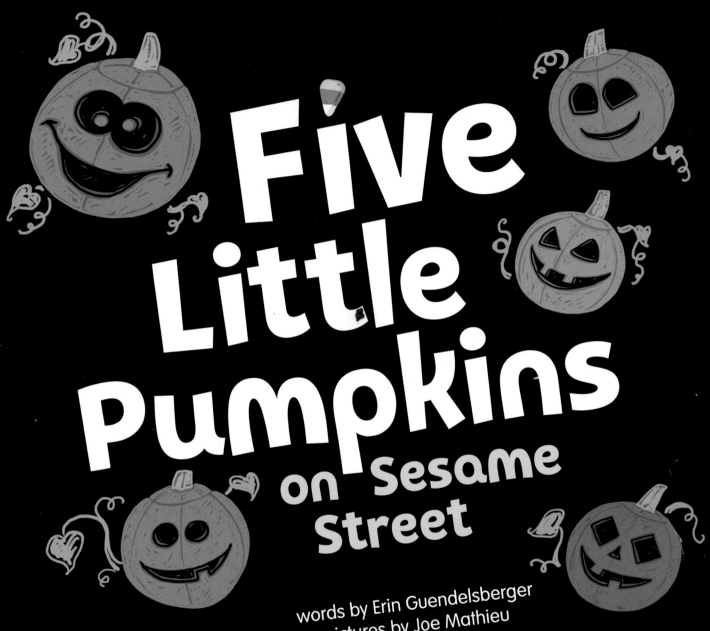

Five Little Pumpkins
on Sesame Street

words by Erin Guendelsberger
pictures by Joe Mathieu

123
SESAME STREET

sourcebooks
wonderland

Five little pumpkins on Sesame Street
were ready to go out and trick-or-treat!

They grabbed their bags, and they skipped out the door,
to meet with their friends at the stoop once more!

A ghost said, "Scram! Stop sitting by my gate!
Go somewhere else to play and celebrate!"

The first one said, "Oh yes, it's getting late!
Me want some candy! Me no can wait!"

The second one said, "There are witches in the air!
Wave hello to the Twiddlebugs, way up there!"

The third one said, "My costume has a tear!
But I shall go on bravely. I do not care!"

The fourth one said, "Let's run and run and run, or let's dance and twirl!" So they leapt and spun!

The fifth one said, "I'm having so much fun!
Did we visit all our neighbors yet, everyone?"

Ooo ooo went the wind, and **out** went the light.
The fourth little pumpkin dropped her basket in fright!

The other pumpkins said, "Zoe, it will be all right," as her Halloween basket rolled out of sight.

Five little pumpkins on Sesame Street,
together shared every Halloween sweet.

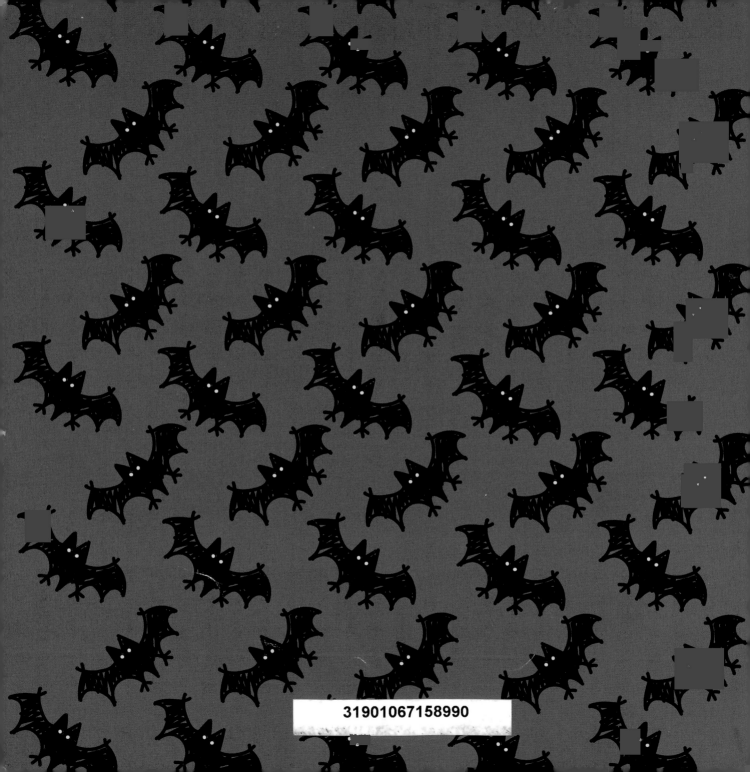